For Isla, Emily and Freya
'With our thoughts, we make the world'

Dedicated to Elsa...
We hope that you are enjoying the view from the stars!

I love my teacher's guts

by
Dr Paul McNamara
Illustrated by **Mike Bastin**

In a rather ordinary and boring school, something extraordinary was about to happen.

Sally and the rest of the class watched as Mrs Trump prepared a special chemistry lesson.

"Children," said Mrs Trump, "when these special chemicals are mixed together, they will cause a memorable explosion! Stand back everyone - a lot of heat and energy is going to be released."

Sally sneaked to the side of the room to get a better view.

With a mix of green and a hue of blue, the bubbling liquid grew and grew. The potion started to fizz, then sizzle, then -

KABOOM......!

An explosion filled the whole room with gas and smoke. Most of the class dived for cover under their desks.

But Sally was propelled through the air like a rocket. As she tumbled through the smoke, she started to feel odd...

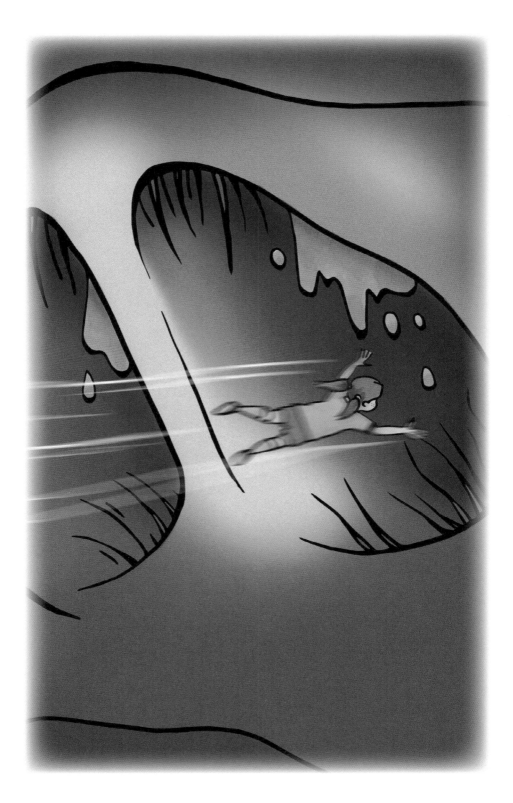

She began to fizzle and crackle until -

FLASH!

- she shrank to the size of a microscopic particle and shot towards her teacher's face!

Sally went straight into Mrs Trump's nose, flying through some of her nose hairs - and got stuck in a web of thick green snot.

"Yuk!" said Sally, "Teacher snot!"

Sally tried to climb out of Mrs Trump's nostril, but the snot blocked her exit. "It's no good - I'm going to have to travel through Mrs Trump," thought Sally.

With a hop, skip and a jump, she slid into
Mrs Trump's oesophagus, the tube that
moves food from Mrs Trump's mouth to her
stomach - and from there, she plummeted
downwards, until ...

SPLASH!

"The stomach is where Mrs Trump digests
her food," thought Sally. "I can't hang
around in this acid for long or I'll be
liquified."

Floating in the green, gurgling liquid was Mrs Trump's breakfast - a Cheerio ring.

"Perfect!" thought Sally. She climbed on, and rode the waves towards the beginning of the small intestine.

Sally surfed the acid sea along the winding seven-metre-long tube that was breaking down Mrs Trump's food into vitamins, minerals and proteins. All these elements would help her body's cells grow and stay healthy.

Up ahead were millions of tiny structures swaying in Mrs Trump's intestine like blades of seaweed in the ocean. "I know what these are - they're called villi," said Sally.

The tiny villi tickled Sally and transported her from Mrs Trump's intestines into her blood vessels. "That was a tight squeeze," thought Sally.

Once inside the blood vessel, she had to dodge hundreds of red and white blood cells that were whooshing past her at great speed. "That just missed taking my head off!" screamed Sally, patting herself down to check she was still in one piece.

Mrs Trump's red blood cells carry oxygen around her body, while her white blood cells are part of her immune system, and help to fight germs called viruses and bacteria.

The white cells started to surround Sally. "I'm under attack," she thought.

Mrs Trump's body was treating Sally like an unwelcome guest. "I'm not meant to be here," said Sally. "Mrs Trump's body thinks I'm the coronavirus! I have to get out of here."

"Ahhh! They're going to swallow me whole," said Sally as a white cell tried to munch her shoe.

KICK - KICK !

"Take that, you menace," Sally yelled as she broke free.

"I need to get out of here."

She grabbed onto a passing red cell and clung on for dear life.

"Whoo-hoo! This is better than my favourite funfair flume," said Sally as she sped through Mrs Trump's bloodstream.

"What is that swooshing noise?" she wondered. .

SWOOSH - SWOOSH - SWOOSH

"I'm headed for Mrs Trump's liver!"

The liver is the largest organ in Mrs Trump's body, and it works like a busy factory, processing the nutrients in her blood, and filtering any waste.

"I feel all shiny and new," thought Sally as she left Mrs Trump's liver.

With a new-found energy and determination to escape, she raced towards Mrs Trump's heart. "Does grumpy old Mrs Trump have a heart?" thought Sally. "It's probably made of stone."

"Only one way to find out!" she said as she sped on.

As she got closer, she could hear….

LUB DUP…LUB DUP…LUB DUP!

- the unmistakable sounds of heart valves opening and closing.

Mrs Trump's heart acts like a magnificent muscular pump that sends blood all around her body and delivers oxygen to her cells.

"She does have a heart after all!" thought Sally.

Sally shot through the chambers of Mrs Trump's heart and into her lungs. "This is where breathing takes place. Mrs Trump's lungs look like big, pink tree branches, with bunches of grapes on them."

Sally grabbed hold of a newly oxygenated red cell, which took her right through the lungs.

Next stop would be Mrs Trump's guts!

The colon is where Mrs Trump makes her poo, and the waste she makes is ejected from her body.

In Mrs Trump's dark, cavernous colon, Sally was overcome by a stifling stench.

"What is that disgusting smell?" said Sally pinching her nose.

"YUKKKK! Teacher poo!"

Sally leapt up and over the smelly excrement. Suddenly, she heard a rumble! The colon started to wiggle, making Sally do a little jig.

Without warning, there was a gigantic gurgle and……..

TRRRUMMMPPPPP!

"I wish Mrs Trump hadn't eaten beans for lunch," said Sally. "You know what they say – 'beans, beans good for your heart, but the more you eat, the more you….

….. FART!'"

Sally shot out of Mrs Trump's butt - and immediately started to fizzle and crackle, and grow back to her normal size.

Sally wiped herself down and said, "That's one science lesson I won't forget in a hurry!"

Could you find your way around the human body?

Sally went on an amazing journey through Mrs Trump's body. It was a bit scary, but very exciting - and she learned so much about all the different parts, what they do, and how they work together.

But can <u>you</u> identify all the main parts of the body in the diagram?

Try covering this left-hand page, and then see if you can name all the parts. *No cheating!*

Good luck!

Brain

Lungs
Heart

Liver
Stomach
Kidneys
Large intestine
Small intestine

Bladder

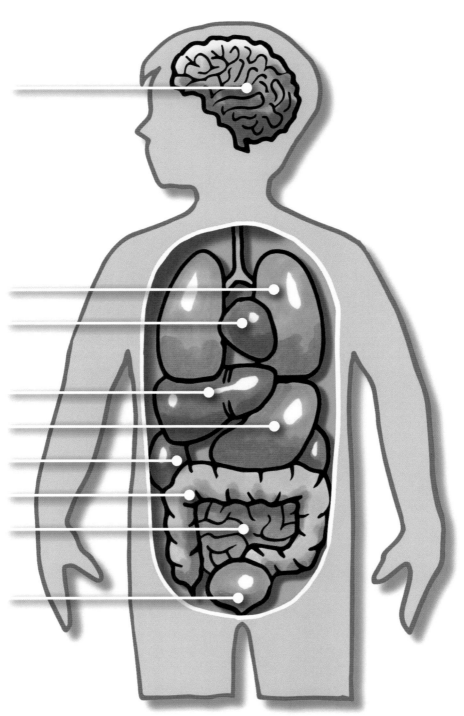